The Missing Manatee

Coral Ripley

For Libby Brown

ORCHARD BOOKS

First published in Great Britain in 2022 by The Watts Publishing Group

1 3 5 7 9 10 8 6 4 2

Text copyright © Orchard Books, 2022
Illustrations copyright © Orchard Books, 2022

A CIP catalogue record for this book
is available from the British Library.

ISBN 978 1 40836 374 4

Printed and bound in Great Britain by Clays Ltd, Elcograf S.p.A.
The paper and board used in this book are made from wood from responsible sources.

Orchard Books
An imprint of
Hachette Children's Group
Part of The Watts Publishing Group Limited
Carmelite House
50 Victoria Embankment
London EC4Y 0DZ

An Hachette UK Company
www.hachette.co.uk
www.hachettechildrens.co.uk

Contents

Chapter One

"This is amazing!" Layla cried. She was standing at the top of some old steep steps that led down to an open-air theatre, a round circular stage surrounded by tall stone pillars that looked like they'd been there for ever. And right behind the stage was the grey-blue sea. A wave came up and splashed against one of the pillars, sending water droplets high into the air.

"Wow!" came a voice from behind Layla. Her two best friends, Emily and Grace, reached the top and gasped at the view.

"I've always wanted to come here," said Layla's mum. "Let's go find our seats." She set off down the stone steps.

"I can't believe your sister is going to be on the stage in front of everyone. I would be so nervous!" Emily said as they all sat down.

"Nadia is a bit nervous," Layla told her. "She's playing Ariel and it's a really big part."

"What's the play about?" Grace asked. "It's called *The Tempest* – that means a storm, right?"

"Oh, I've got a programme you can look at." Layla's mum handed it along.

"I know all about it; I've been

 9

helping Nadia learn her lines," Layla explained. "It's about a magician who gets shipwrecked on an island with his daughter, Miranda, a spirit called Ariel and a monster called Caliban. It's by Shakespeare so it's all in funny old language, but it's really dramatic." She took a deep breath and flung her arm out to point at the sea, reciting: "Full fathom five your father lies, of his bones are coral made!" The others giggled. Layla loved performing – she should be on stage too!

"You're going to have to be an actress when you grow up," Emily laughed.

Layla sighed. "I would love to be. But I'm so bad at reading the lines." She glanced at the programme to look for her sister's name, but as usual the letters were all jumbled around. She gave a deep sigh.

Her mum reached over and squeezed her hand. "Lots of actors are dyslexic, darling."

"Are they?" Layla said in surprise.

Her mum nodded. "Some actors get someone to record their lines and they learn them by listening to them. Your dyslexia won't stop you doing anything you want – you just might have to be a bit creative in how you do it."

"I'll read your lines for you!" Emily offered.

"Me too!" Grace agreed.

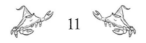

Layla grinned at her friends, then looked at the stage again. Maybe she would be an actress after all!

The theatre was filling up with excited chatter. Suddenly there was an *ooh* as someone ran on to the stage. She had long dark hair like Layla and was

wearing sparkly face paint and beautiful blue fairy wings.

"Nadia!" Layla gasped.

Nadia gave a deep curtsey that

made the bottom of her wings brush the ground.

"Ladies and gentlemen, boys and girls," she announced loudly. "Welcome to the Cliffside Theatre for our production of *The Tempest*! By the looks of the grey clouds, it's likely we'll get some rain during the performance, so anoraks are available at the kiosk, along with snacks and drinks. The show will start in ten minutes!" She bowed again and ran off, as light on her feet as if she really were flying.

"Here." Layla's mum passed down some money. "I've got an umbrella; you girls go and get yourselves an anorak each."

"Thanks, Mum!" Layla said. The girls stood up and shuffled along the row back to the stairs. The clouds overhead were getting darker and the waves were looking really rough now. They ran up to the kiosk and joined the queue.

"I hope Marina is safe at Atlantis," Emily murmured as she looked at the stormy sea.

The girls exchanged a secret grin. Princess Marina was their special friend – their mermaid friend! When Emily had moved to their seaside town, they'd saved a dolphin trapped in a fishing net. But Kai was no ordinary dolphin – he was the pet of a mermaid princess! After they'd helped Kai, Marina had brought them to the kingdom of Atlantis and they'd become Sea Keepers, special guardians of the sea.

"It would be fun to swim in those giant waves, though!" Grace said. "It would be like surfing, but underwater!"

Layla thought about being a Sea Keeper as she peered at the queue of people lined up to get plastic anoraks. Their main job was to find the powerful Golden Pearls before the evil siren, Effluvia, could get them. Whenever the Mystic Clam remembered the location of another pearl, Marina would call the Sea Keepers on their magical shell bracelets. Layla smiled as she fiddled with the beautiful purple shell bracelet she always wore. On their underwater adventures, they'd learnt loads about how human rubbish was hurting the sea. As the couple in front of them shook out their new plastic coats, Layla turned to her friends.

"I don't think those anoraks are a good idea," she said. "People will use them once then put them in the bin, and they'll stay in a rubbish tip for hundreds of years."

Emily nodded. "It would be awful if they got into the sea. Remember when we met the sea turtles? Lots of them eat plastic bags thinking they're jellyfish."

"Let's just get wet!" Grace said, raising her arms up to the rain. "Whenever it's raining my grandad says: 'You're not made of sugar, you won't melt!'"

The others giggled as they left the queue. The rain started to come down, pittering and pattering on their faces. "We should say: 'We don't mind getting wet, after all we're mermaids!'" Emily said.

Layla grinned as she started to walk back up the steps. Holding the handrail, she noticed something amazing – her shell bracelet was glowing, and so were Emily's and Grace's!

"Marina needs us!" Emily gasped.

They quickly ducked behind the kiosk.

"Please take your seats. The performance will start in five minutes," an announcement rang out. The girls

grinned. Time passed differently in the mermaid world; they could have a whole adventure and be back before the play began!

Holding hands, they said the words Marina had taught them:

"Take me to the ocean blue,

Sea Keepers to the rescue!"

The raindrops started whizzing around them, faster and faster in a magical whirlwind. Another mermaid adventure was about to begin!

Chapter Two

"Wahoo! We're mermaids again!" Grace yelled, kicking her yellow fins and diving down deep into the warm green water.

Layla reached down to pat her aquamarine tail, stroking the tiny scales and flicking her light pink fins. It was so wonderful to have her tail back!

"Marina!" Emily called as she spotted the mermaid princess swimming over to

them with her arms open wide.

"Hello, Sea Keepers!" Marina called delightedly as the girls all swam over for a big group hug. Layla laughed as the princess's pink and purple hair spread through the water and tickled her face.

"Where are we this time?" Grace asked.

Layla looked around. The water was as warm as a bath and so shallow that she could easily see down to the bottom.

"We're in the Straits of Florida," Marina explained. "The Mystic Clam remembered that there might be another Golden Pearl near here."

"Ooh, I've always wanted to visit Florida," Layla said.

The Mystic Clam was the only creature old enough to remember where Marina's ancestor, Queen Nerissa, had hidden the Golden Pearls. It was up to the Sea Keepers to find them and use their magic for good before the wicked siren Effluvia could get them and use their power for evil.

"What did the Mystic Clam say?" Grace asked.

"It's a bit of a strange riddle," Marina admitted. She cleared her throat and recited:

"Where roots take hold in the salty sea,
The pearl lies hidden by an ancient tree."

"A tree? I've never seen a tree

underwater," Grace said in confusion.

"Maybe it could be a type of seaweed?" Layla suggested.

As they were trying to figure it out, there was a roaring sound from the surface. Emily ducked down nervously.

"A swamp boat!" Marina shouted.

The mermaids quickly dived down as it passed overhead, its sharp propeller cutting through the water.

"Those blades are very dangerous," Marina said, her voice drowned out by the growling engine.

Layla noticed a shadow up ahead, floating exactly where the boat was heading. She scrunched up her eyes,

but it was too far away to see clearly. "What's that?" she asked, pointing it out to her friends.

"I don't know, but the boat is going straight towards it!" Grace said in alarm. "Come on!"

The Sea Keepers kicked their fins and powered forward, swimming as fast as they could. Layla peered through the water as she swam, straining to see. As they got closer, the shape got clearer and clearer – it was a creature the size of Grace's dog, Barkley. It looked a bit like a seal, but very round and tubby. It was staring straight at the boat curiously, but it wasn't moving out of the way!

"It's a baby manatee!" Marina said.

"Little manatee!" Emily called. "Watch out!" But the manatee still didn't move – and the boat was heading right for it, its sharp propellers whirling and roaring, slicing through the water. If the manatee didn't move, it was going to get badly hurt!

"We're not going to make it," Marina gasped.

"Yes, we are!" Grace said. She put on another burst of speed, like she was trying to win one of her swimming races, and pushed ahead of the others. Just in time she put her hands out and grabbed the manatee around its middle, pulling it

out of the way and diving down after it.
A split second later, the boat roared over
where they'd just been.

Phew! Layla breathed a sigh of relief
as they all crowded around the little
creature. "Well done, Grace!"

"Didn't you see the swamp boat?" Emily
asked the manatee.

"Oh, was that what that was!" the
manatee exclaimed. "I've never seen a
boat like that before."

"Yes, and they're very dangerous,"
Marina scolded the little creature. "You
could have been really hurt."

"I'm sorry," the manatee said in her
soft, sweet voice. "I didn't know it was

dangerous. It was making such an interesting noise!" She tried to copy the roaring of the boat and the girls giggled. The little manatee was so cute!

"I'm Silva," the baby manatee introduced herself.

"I'm Layla. This is Marina, Grace and Emily," Layla told her. "We've never met a manatee before."

"Nice to meet you! My herd is just

over there," Silva said. "We're about
to start our migration. Every year we
migrate all the way to warmer water in
South America. It's my first trip and it's
suuuuuuch a long way! Granny says I'm
going to have to swim fast to keep up
and not wander off. But today will be
so much fun – lots of creatures come for
a farewell party to wave us off." Silva
gasped like she had just had a great idea.
"Would you like to come? We'd love to
have you!"

Layla glanced at her friends. Emily
looked as excited as Layla felt – she
was probably thinking she could learn
loads about a new animal. Grace was

frowning. Layla guessed she was thinking about finding the Golden Pearl.

"I know we have to get the pearl but we can't miss a party!" Layla said. "Besides, maybe the manatees could help us solve the riddle?

"Oh, we love riddles," Silva said. "I'm sure we can help."

Layla grinned at her friends, who grinned back. They were off to a manatee party!

Chapter Three

"My herd is just this way," Silva said.
The girls followed the baby manatee as
she led them towards the shore, but she
was going so slowly that it was hard to
swim behind her. Grace kept darting
ahead and coming back impatiently, but
Silva didn't seem to notice. She drifted
along, stopping to sniff at the shallow
coral reef or nibble on some sea grass.

"Would you like some?" Silva offered Layla, with her mouth full of grass.

"Oh, no thanks!" Layla said. "People don't eat grass."

"Really?" Silva said in surprise. "So what do you eat?"

"Humans eat all kinds of things," Emily explained. "My family have a café and we make lots of cakes and breads and delicious treats."

"My favourite is water lettuce," Silva said. "Granny says there will be loads in South America."

"Look, is that the farewell party?" Layla pointed up ahead.

"I'll go and find out!" Grace said. With

34

a flick of her tail, she was off. Before they'd made it much closer, she was back, looking excited. "There are loads of manatees and mermaids, but lots of other creatures too! Come on!" Grace turned and sped off, the others following her.

As they got nearer, they could see Grace was right. There were mermaids everywhere, all wearing party hats made out of seaweed. The seabed was laid out with an enormous picnic with all kinds of food piled high. Lots of creatures were gathered around eating and chatting happily.

"Ooh look, Atlantic blue crabs!" Marina said excitedly. "And those are red snapper fish just arriving."

Silva went slightly faster as she approached a huge manatee with white whiskers and a broad speckled back. "Granny!" she called out. The grey manatee turned and opened her flippers for a hug. Silva swam up to her and the two manatees rubbed noses. "Why, Silva, where have you been?" she asked in a slow drawl.

"I made some friends, Granny," Silva explained, introducing them.

"Hello!" the elderly manatee said, "I'm Silva's granny, but you can call me Valeria."

"Right, manatees, if we could just go

a little bit faster . . ." a nearby mermaid
called.

Valeria turned to them and winked.
"Tia is always hustling and bustling us,"
she said.

"What's the hurry?" another manatee
complained.

Tia, a mermaid with a black tail
and curly brown hair, swam over. "I'm
sorry to rush you, but there's a storm
approaching, and I want you to set off
on your journey before it hits." She swam
away to gather the rest of the herd.

Silva and Valeria headed slowly up to
the surface to breathe.

"We'd better check out this storm,"

Marina said. The girls nodded, and they all followed the manatees to the surface.

As she burst into the air and shook her wet hair out of her eyes, Layla gasped. There were huge dark storm clouds on the horizon. They made the clouds over the theatre look tiny.

Emily gulped. "Tia was right, there's a big storm coming."

"Well, once we find the Golden Pearl we can use its magic to give the manatees a safe migration," Layla declared, sounding much more confident than she felt inside.

They dived back down to the herd and helped Tia hustle the manatees along

into a group. They gathered in the
shallow water next to the shore, chatting
excitedly.

"Princess Marina, would you do us the
honour of starting the farewell song?" Tia
asked, offering them all party hats.

Marina blushed, but gave a regal nod

of her head. "I'd be delighted."

She opened her mouth and sang, her beautiful mermaid voice lilting through the still water.

"Welcome all, friends, sons and daughters,
To wish this herd of manatees
A safe journey and calm waters—"

"GATOR!" Tia screamed, and everyone panicked.

A giant alligator had slid from the land down into the water. It had a huge knobbly, scaly head, yellow eyes, and looked like a hungry dinosaur as it swam towards the party, licking its lips.

"Is that a crocodile?" Grace gasped at the huge beast.

Emily shook her head. "It's an alligator; they have broader snouts. They're really dangerous and even eat people. They grab them and pull them underwater in a death roll." She shuddered.

"They don't normally eat mermaids or manatees," Marina said. "But look at its yellow eyes. This one is under a spell!"

Sure enough, the alligator was heading right for the manatees, its jaws open wide. The manatees were fleeing as fast as they could – but that wasn't very quick at all.

"Get away from them!" Tia yelled bravely, using her fins to kick dust from the seabed up at the scaly beast.

While Marina and Emily hurried the manatees away, Grace and Layla swam over to join Tia. They used their tails to flick up sand and debris from the seabed, making the water too murky for the

alligator to see through.

The enchanted alligator shook its scaly head and snapped its jaws viciously, but there was nothing it could do.

"Link arms!" Tia yelled. All the mermaids joined their arms together and made a ring around the manatees, facing out to stare down the hypnotised reptile.

Through the dust, Layla could see the glowing yellow eyes of the alligator as it swam away. It was definitely under a spell – and Layla could bet who had enchanted it . . . Effluvia! She looked around everywhere, but she couldn't see any sign of the evil siren.

The alligator's tail disappeared into

the murky water and the mermaid next to her gave a cheer. As the mermaids around her relaxed, Layla felt her heart calm down. The threat was gone.

"What a scare!" Tia declared with relief. "Thanks for your help!"

The manatees started laughing and

chatting as they prepared to set off. But then one voice came above the crowd. "Silva!" Valeria called out worriedly. "Where's my Silva?"

Chapter Four

As they searched for the baby manatee, a familiar laugh burbled through the water. Effluvia!

"A party, for *me*? You shouldn't have!" A beautiful mermaid with long midnight blue hair gave a tinkling laugh as she swam out of the dust. She swished her dark purple tail through the water, like a cat about to pounce.

"The alligator was the perfect distraction!" Effluvia laughed again. "And now I have exactly what I want – a manatee of my own!"

"My Silva!" Valeria gasped. "She's taken my granddaughter!"

"Don't worry, we won't let her hurt Silva," Emily promised.

"We've stopped her before, we'll stop her again," Grace added fiercely.

"So you might as well just tell us where she is now!" Layla agreed.

"Tut, tut, tut, Sea Keepers, I'm the one in charge here," Effluvia drawled. "That is, if you ever want to see your sea cow friend again."

"What do you want, Effluvia?" Marina asked defiantly.

"Why, what I always want!" Effluvia acted surprised. "A Golden Pearl so I can free my siren sisters and take over Atlantis for good!"

"That's not going to happen!" Grace declared.

"Oh, but it will," Effluvia spat, looking deadly serious. "And YOU are going to find it for me. Once I have it, I'll give Silva back to her herd. Why should I do all the hard work when you two-legs are here to do it for me!"

As Valeria sobbed, Marina and the girls turned to comfort her. "It's OK, we will rescue Silva," Layla promised her.

"But we can't give Effluvia a Golden Pearl," Grace whispered.

Marina shook her head. "No. She and her siren sisters would destroy Atlantis and then even more creatures would be in danger."

"But we can't leave Silva in danger either. We made a Sea Keeper promise to help all sea creatures!" Emily reminded the others in a low voice.

Layla, Grace and Emily exchanged worried glances. What were they going to do?

"Talk amongst yourselves, don't mind me!" Effluvia called. "There's nothing you can do! I've won this time!"

"We can't just take your word that Silva is safe," Emily called back. "Show us that she's OK."

Effluvia sighed. "Fine, fine," she snapped, rolling her eyes.

The siren began to sing and the girls immediately covered their ears. Effluvia's magical singing was how she cast powerful spells to hypnotise creatures and make them do whatever she wanted.

As Effluvia sang, a huge bubble appeared, bobbing in the water next to her. In it, they could see their little manatee friend, looking sad and scared.

"My Silva!" Valeria cried out.

Layla looked at the bubble, trying to get any clues about where Effluvia was keeping the manatee. She hoped to spot a colourful shell or plant or a landmark of some kind. But there was nothing except water surrounding their manatee friend, and the enchanted alligator hungrily circling around her.

"We HAVE to save Silva," Emily said. Layla and Grace nodded.

"We'll get the pearl, but you have to promise to let Silva go," Layla said.

"Cross my fins and hope to cry," Effluvia said sweetly. She gave a satisfied smile and tossed her hair. "I knew I'd get my way," she laughed. "Now off you go

and don't come back without my pearl."
She swam over to the picnic and started
eating the party food.

"You can't give her the pearl," Marina
whispered, looking pale. "I can't let you."

"We won't," promised Layla. "But Silva
will be safe while we look for it. And
it will give us time to think of another
plan."

"Keep protecting the manatees," Grace
said to Tia in a low voice. "We can't
trust Effluvia and we have to keep them
safe."

Tia nodded but looked up at the surface
anxiously. The water was getting very
choppy. "We'll look after them," she

promised, "but you don't have long – the storm is coming."

"What was the riddle again?" Grace asked.

"*Where roots take hold in the salty sea,*
The pearl lies hidden by an ancient tree," Marina recited.

"Does anyone know what that means?" Layla asked the manatees. They shook their grey heads.

"A tree is most likely to be near the shore," Emily thought out loud.

"There's a forest of mangrove trees, that way." One of the manatees pointed a flipper.

"Great!" Grace said. "Come on, we can

55

work out how to save Silva as we go."

One of the manatees pushed to
the front. "I'm coming too!" Valeria
said firmly. "I'm going to rescue my
granddaughter and bring her back home.
Besides, no one knows these swampy
waters like I do."

Valeria looked at the Sea Keepers
as if she was daring them to disagree.
Layla went over and put her arm around
Valeria's speckled back. "Good. We need
all the help we can get!"

Chapter Five

"Come on, Valeria," Marina called back as the elderly manatee swam slowly along. Old manatees were even slower than baby ones!

"We should have told her to stay with the others!" Grace grumbled.

"*Ssssh!*" Emily whispered. "She wanted to help her granddaughter!"

"I want to save Silva too. That's why

we have to hurry!" Grace said.

"Why don't you and Marina scout on ahead?" Layla suggested.

Grace and Marina took off straight away, following the shore and keeping their eyes open for any sign of the tree roots in the riddle.

"Oh Valeria, let me help you!" Emily said as she spotted that Valeria had stopped to eat some sea grass. She quickly pulled it up and held it out for Valeria to nibble as she swam along. They still weren't going fast but at least they were moving!

"You girls are just so kind!" Valeria said with a smile.

"Emily! Layla!" Grace shouted from up ahead. "We've found something!"

"You girls go, I'll catch up," Valeria said. "My old flippers aren't what they used to be." Emily and Layla sped off after their friend. Grace and Marina were

waiting near the shore. Long, thick tree roots were stretching into the water like bony fingers.

"Where roots take hold in the salty sea!" Grace said delightedly.

Emily shuddered. "They're sort of creepy," she said.

"And there are so many of them," Marina pointed out. "How are we ever going to find which one of them is the ancient tree in the riddle?"

Layla looked round at the tree roots, which were spread out like an underwater forest. There were creatures everywhere:

tiny crabs scuttling about the roots, jellyfish bobbing nearby and little fish darting in and out, snacking on algae.

"Oh dearie me." Valeria huffed and puffed as she swam up to them. "I haven't been here in a month of Sundays. When I was a tiny manatee, my brother and I used to play hide and seek here."

"Do you know which one is the ancient tree?" Layla asked her.

Valeria looked around. "There was one tree . . ." she said thoughtfully. "It was old even when I was younger than Silva is now. Its roots formed a cave that was the perfect hiding place . . ."

"Where is it?" Grace asked eagerly.

"Oh." Valeria tapped her flippers together. "I'm not sure. I know it was deep among the mangroves . . . But there are so many more now than there used to be, and my memory isn't what it was . . ." She trailed off, looking like she was about to cry. "Oh, my Silva is waiting to be rescued and silly old me can't remember where that tree was!"

"It's OK." Emily patted her flipper reassuringly. "You've been so helpful – and there are five of us, we can all look. I'm sure we'll find an old tree with roots like a cave."

Valeria brightened up and Grace quickly got them organised. "I'll go round the left-hand side. Marina, you go to the right. Layla, head to the surface, and Emily, swim underneath. Valeria, swim straight through and we'll all meet in the middle. If you spot the ancient tree, shout as loud as you can and the others can follow your voice."

Everyone nodded. Layla kicked her fins and swam though the jungle of tree roots. Even without Valeria she still couldn't go that fast – the twisty roots twirled and tangled through the water. *Emily was right,* she thought, *they* are *creepy.* They reminded her of arms with outstretched fingers ready to grab you! One trailed through her hair. "Eek!" Layla squealed, then shook herself. They were just tree roots! Still, she was glad she was going to the surface. She swam up, weaving though the roots and out into the light.

As she put her head out of the water Layla blinked in the sunshine. It was so bright and hot after being underwater, even though the huge black clouds were still hovering nearby, threatening to pour with rain. She looked around at the trees, trying to spot the ancient one. Just then, some movement caught her eye. There was something perched in the green leaves of a nearby mangrove tree – a big brown bird with a white neck and a yellow head. But the strangest thing about it was its huge beak. "Is that a pelican?" Layla asked herself. Emily would know for sure!

"Hello, could you help me? I'm looking for an ancient tree," she said, splashing

her tail as she swam through the water towards it. The pelican didn't reply but flapped its wings anxiously.

"I won't hurt you," Layla said. "I'm a Sea Keeper – I made a promise to protect all sea creatures. And I could do with your help to save a little manatee …" But the pelican still didn't answer. Instead, he flapped even more as she got closer.

"Are you OK?" Layla said, suddenly realising that the pelican was acting oddly. The bird started dragging his beak across the branches, like he was scratching an itch – or trying to get something off.

"Oh, you've got something stuck on your beak!" Layla gasped as she saw it glinting in the sunshine.

She swam over and pulled herself up into the tree, tucking her tail into the tangle of roots, then reached as high as she could. The pelican flinched as she got closer, but he didn't fly away. "I promise, I just want to help," Layla said.

The pelican had something wrapped around his beak, holding it tightly shut. It was like wire, but clear. "I think it's a fishing line," Layla said. It was digging in painfully, and the pelican's beak was scuffed and scratched from where he had been trying to get it off. "You poor thing, this must hurt," she muttered, looking into the pelican's beady black eye. The pelican nodded and Layla stroked his tufty yellow head. "I'll untangle you, don't worry," she said as she picked at the string with her nails.

She picked and pulled at the fishing wire, and eventually she was able to start unwinding it. It came away fast, and soon the pelican was free.

"Done!" Layla cried joyfully. The pelican immediately swooped down to the water and took a long drink, the water filling up his special beak and gulping down his throat.

"Phew, that's better!" he said. "Thank

you so much. I thought I would never get it off! My name is Beaky."

"I'm Layla," Layla said. "I'm really sorry you got tangled in the wire," she added guiltily. "It shouldn't have been left in the water. But not all humans are bad. My friends and I are Sea Keepers who want to help sea creatures. We're looking for an ancient tree, do you know where it is?"

Beaky scratched his head with his wingtip. "There *is* one tree that's been around since my grandparents were eggs," he said. "That might be the one you're looking for. I'll show you!"

"Oh, thank you!" Layla cried. "Hang

on!" She slid off the tree roots and down into the water below. "Everyone," she yelled at the top of her voice. "I've found something, this way!" Layla kept calling as one by one her friends appeared,

following the sound of her voice.

They weaved around the trees, following Beaky as he flew high above. He kept perching on the mangrove trees and calling, "Not far now!"

There were so many roots that it was difficult to swim. "This is impossible!" Marina complained.

There was a flurry of feathers and leaves and the pelican landed in the mangrove bush next to them. "It's just up ahead." He pointed his wing up on to the dry land.

"The tide is out!" Valeria cried. "We can't swim there until the water is higher and the mangroves flood. Oh, my poor

Silva!" she sobbed.

"Don't worry!" Grace told her. "We can still get to the tree!"

"Marina, can you turn us back to humans?" Layla cried

"Of course!" Marina grinned.

"We'll be right back," promised Emily, patting Valeria reassuringly.

Marina cleared her throat, then sang a high song in her beautiful mermaid voice.

"Send the Sea Keepers back to land,
We need the girls to lend a hand."

Magical colours spread out in the water and swirled around their tails, surrounding them with bubbles that

73

popped and fizzed. "That tickles!" giggled Layla. She wriggled her tail and realised that it had transformed back into her legs. She was wearing a bright green spotty swimming costume. Grace's bathing suit was covered in blue stars and Emily's was stripy pink.

"Well, I never!" Valeria gasped as she looked at their legs in amazement.

The girls scrambled to their feet and set off, splashing through the water and climbing over the twisted branches.

"Follow that pelican!" Layla yelled.

Chapter Six

Grace held out a hand and helped her friends clamber over a knobbly mangrove root. Layla shaded her eyes as she stared up through the branches, looking out for a sign of Beaky.

"There he is," Emily said, pointing. Beaky landed heavily on the branches of a tree just ahead and squawked. They could see his beak moving, but no words

were coming out, just noises.

"Of course!" Grace sighed. "We can't understand him anymore because we don't have our mermaid tails."

Beaky squawked again and shook his wings.

"Sorry, we don't understand," Emily said. "But maybe we can work it out? Are we nearly at the ancient tree?"

This time, Beaky nodded and the girls grinned at each other.

"Great! Can you see it from here?" Layla asked. Beaky shook his feathers and started squawking insistently. What was he trying to say?

"You can't see the tree, but we're near

76

it?" Layla guessed. Beaky nodded again.

"OK. Can you still take us there?" Grace asked. "Maybe once we're there we'll understand what he means?" she added to her friends.

With one more nod, Beaky took off. The girls stumbled through the mangrove bushes and out into a clearing. The ground was much drier here and there weren't as many trees, just lots of stumps where the mangroves had been cut down.

"I thought Valeria said the tree was in the middle of the forest," Emily said, looking around. The ground was muddy and barren, and there were dead tree stumps everywhere. Grace ran over to stand on one to see if she could see anything. "I think that once this was the middle of the forest," she said. "It's just all been chopped down."

Beaky was flying in circles overhead.

"That's why he couldn't see the ancient tree!" Layla realised suddenly. "It's been cut down."

"Humans again," Emily said sadly. "People cut down the trees for firewood or to make farmland."

The girls looked around in dismay. Unlike the underwater trees they'd passed on their way, there weren't any creatures bustling among the dead tree roots. All those animals had lost their homes when the trees had been cut down.

"If the ancient tree's gone, how will we find the pearl?" Grace wondered.

"The riddle mentioned roots, didn't it?" Layla said, looking at the stumpy trees. "And the roots are still here. Maybe there's still a chance we can find it."

Beaky perched on the biggest tree stump. It was so wide that all three girls could have laid down on it like an enormous bed. "You can tell how old a tree is by how many rings it has in its trunk," Emily said, running her finger along the circles in the tree stump. There were far too many to count. "This tree really was ancient. Thousands of years old."

"And look, its roots are like a cave!" Grace said, disappearing under them.

"This must be the one!"

Layla felt a pull of sadness as she wondered how long the tree had been in the forest until people had come along. But she pushed those thoughts away – the dark clouds overhead were getting even closer, and the manatees had to leave before the storm came!

"I wish we had some spades or something," Grace said as she started to dig down among the roots. Layla grabbed a stick and started scratching at the soft mud, revealing more of the ancient roots buried deep underground.

The girls dug and dug, pulling up more of the sticky mud, looking out for any glint of golden pearl. Meanwhile, Beaky flew around searching for oysters.

"What are we going to do if we find it?" Layla thought out loud. "No matter what, we can't give it to Effluvia. She'd do all kinds of awful things with it. But we have to save Silva!"

"Maybe we could just use the pearl's power to wish Silva free?" Emily suggested, wiping mud down her swimming costume.

"But then we couldn't help the herd with the rest of the migration," Grace said with a sigh. She'd been digging furiously and her face was streaked with mud.

"First we have to find it!" Emily said.
She scrambled over a root and slipped.
"Whoops!"

"Are you OK?" Layla and Grace rushed
to help their friend.

Emily was lying face-down in the mud.
Layla tried not to giggle as Emily sat up,

covered in the squelchy brown muck. But to their surprise she wasn't upset – she had an enormous smile on her face.

"Look!" Emily showed them something buried in the tree root where she'd fallen. A magical glow was coming from the mud. The girls gasped in excitement and all started digging together. Seconds later Layla's fingers touched something smooth and warm and glowing with magic – the Golden Pearl!

"Yes!" cried Emily.

"We've got the pearl, now we need to work out what to do with it!" Grace said. They looked up at the black clouds hovering overhead.

"The manatees will probably be OK if we wish Silva free . . ." Grace said, looking up at the ominous storm clouds uncertainly.

As they sat and thought, Beaky shook his feathers and flew off, coming back a few moments later with an oyster shell. He dropped three more at the girls' feet.

"Oh, thank you," Emily said, "but I don't eat oysters."

Layla agreed. "Um, I think you can have these, Beaky," she said.

Beaky gave a squawk and expertly opened the oyster shell with a flick of his beak. In the middle was a white pearl.

"Oh look!" Layla gasped. She picked

the pearl up and showed the others.

"If only that one was magic too, that would solve everything!" Grace joked.

As Layla held the white pearl in one hand and the Golden Pearl in the other, she had an idea. The pearl didn't have to be magic, it just had to *look* magic – like Nadia's fairy wings or the other props in the play. She turned to her friends, grinning widely. "I have a plan!"

Chapter Seven

"We're going to trick Effluvia by acting!" Layla said excitedly.

"Acting?" Grace asked.

Emily pulled a face. "But I can't act!"

"Yes, you can!" Layla tried to convince her. "And besides, it won't be like acting on a stage in front of lots of people. All we have to do is act like we don't want to give Effluvia the Golden Pearl."

"But we don't want to give her the Golden Pearl," Grace said.

"Exactly!" Layla grinned. "We won't give her the Golden Pearl, we'll give her this one!" She held out the white pearl instead. Grace and Emily stared at it. It was about the right size and shape, but it was completely the wrong colour.

"Um, I think she might notice the difference," Emily said.

"I'm sure Marina can use her mermaid magic to make it gold," Layla said. "And if we act well enough, Effluvia won't look too closely at the pearl. You know Effluvia, she'll be too busy laughing and gloating . . ." Layla threw her head back and cackled, doing a brilliant impression of the evil siren. "I knew you stupid two-legs would never defeat ME! Mwah ha ha ha!"

Grace giggled, but Emily still looked nervous. "I know you can act, Layla, but I can't! What if Effluvia figures it out?"

"We only need to distract her for long enough to save Silva and use the Golden Pearl's magic to help the manatees," Layla said.

"It's the best plan we've got," Grace said, shrugging.

They both turned to Emily. "OK . . ." she said reluctantly. "I'll try my best!"

"Thank you for all your help," Layla called to Beaky, who was still happily eating the oysters, his big beak wobbling as he swallowed them whole.

Grace glanced at the heavy grey storm

clouds above them. "We'd better hurry. We're running out of time."

The girls headed out of the clearing, jumping over the tree roots and squelching though the mud. The tide was coming in now, and the water was pooling around the trees, making it even harder to walk. It seemed to take ages, but eventually they could see Marina and Valeria waiting up ahead. The mermaid waved her hands excitedly, and the manatee waved a flipper.

"Did you get it?" Marina asked.

"Yes!" Layla said breathlessly, tripping over a root and landing with a loud splash in front of her mermaid friend.

"But now we need your help!"

Quickly Layla explained her plan. Marina looked at the white pearl and nodded. "I should be able to do that," she said. "But the magic won't last long."

"That's OK," Layla told her. "We just need long enough to rescue Silva!"

"But first we need to find her . . ." Grace said.

"Actually, first I need to give you your tails back," Marina said with a grin. "Otherwise you'll be swimming even slower than a manatee!"

Marina quickly sang the magical song to turn them back into mermaids. Rainbow colours swirled through the

water and suddenly
they had their
mermaid tails
again!

"Wahoo!"
Grace cheered,
diving deep
into the water
to wash off all
the mud. Layla and
Emily followed. Layla kicked her fins
delightedly as she felt the cool water
whoosh around her tail.

But there was no time to have fun.
Layla took one look at Valeria's worried
face and swam over to her friends. "Come

on, let's go find Silva," she said.

"Goodness only knows where she is," Valeria fretted. "To think she's stuck with that hungry alligator circling her! Oh dearie me!"

As the girls rushed to comfort her, Layla thought about what they'd seen in the magic bubble.

"What clues did we get from the magic bubble?" she asked.

"Nothing," Marina said. "There was water rushing past . . ."

". . . and the alligator swimming round and round Silva," Grace added. Valeria gave a moan.

"But that doesn't help! There's water

94

and alligators everywhere!" Layla sighed.

"Actually . . ." Emily said thoughtfully.

The others turned to look at her.

"Alligators live in fresh water, not the sea," Emily continued. "They can only come a little way into the saltwater."

"That's right," Valeria added. "They live in rivers. Whenever they do come into the sea they stay close to the shore."

"OK!" said Grace excitedly. "So that's a clue!"

"And the water was flowing all around her, like a river," Emily added.

"Where's the nearest river, Valeria?" Marina asked.

"The Crystal River!" Valeria

exclaimed. She kicked her flippers and started moving as fast as she could. "Follow me!"

Valeria led them along, dodging the trailing mangrove roots but always keeping the shore on their left-hand side. As they went, Layla came up with a plan for convincing Effluvia. "I'll do most of the talking," she reassured Emily. "Just pretend that you don't want me to give her the pearl."

Suddenly the shore disappeared and they could feel the rush of water coming towards them. "This is the mouth of the river!" Marina said. "It's show time."

"I have butterflies in my tummy!"

Emily said. "I don't know how Nadia went on stage in front of all those people. I'm nervous enough just acting in front of one person."

"One horrible, scary mermaid," Grace said. "But we have to do it – for Silva!"

A determined look came over Emily's face and she nodded. Emily would do anything to help an animal – even if she was scared.

"Here, you'll need this." Marina held out the pearl and closed her eyes as she started to sing.

"Mermaid magic deep and old,
Make this plain white pearl glow gold!"

Magic swirled around the pearl and

surrounded it with glittering light. The pearl transformed from white to gold.

Layla carefully gave the real Golden Pearl to Grace for safe-keeping. Then she took the fake golden pearl and hid it behind her back. It didn't feel as old and magical as the Golden Pearl, and it wasn't glowing as brightly, but hopefully Effluvia wouldn't notice the difference – at least until she tried to use its power!

"Good luck," Marina said. "Flip a fin – that's what mermaids say to actors before they go onstage!"

Her tummy bubbling with nerves, Layla led her friends into the river. The water was flowing around them and it tasted fresh and clear, not salty like the sea.

"Look out for Silva," Grace said as they went. "She must be here somewhere."

"Listen! What's that?" Emily asked. It sounded like talking.

As they got closer, they saw Silva chatting animatedly to the alligator. "What's your favourite colour? And what do you like better – sea lettuce or sea grass?" The alligator groaned and shook its head as the little manatee asked question after question.

"Sea Keepers!" Silva said delightedly as she saw them swimming over. "Have you come to rescue me? I knew you would! I've been waiting for you with my new friend. Where did you go?" asked Silva. "I want to hear all about it."

But the alligator obviously didn't. Rolling its yellow eyes, it swam away. Had the friendly little manatee worn it down with all her chatter?

Layla looked around. There was no sign of Effluvia. "Maybe we can sneak Silva away without giving Effluvia the pearl?" Emily said hopefully.

"Come on, Silva, let's get you back to your herd," Emily said, putting an arm around her. "Your granny has been so worried about you."

"NOT SO FAST," a voice boomed. They turned to see a siren with her hands on her hips, glaring at them furiously. It was Effluvia!

Chapter Eight

"Did you really think you could take the manatee without giving me the pearl?" Effluvia snarled. "Hand it over!"

The alligator was back too, and it wasn't alone. Glowing yellow eyes surrounded Effluvia, followed by long scaly snouts and sharp teeth.

"Give. Me. That. Pearl," Effluvia demanded, holding out her hand.

Layla could see Emily shaking as she
held on tightly to Silva, who was scared
into silence by the ravenous alligators all
around them.

"It's OK, Emily," Layla said, giving
her a wink. Emily gave a tiny nod and
squeezed Silva's flipper.

Then Layla swam forward, holding out

the fake Golden Pearl.

Effluvia looked at it greedily. "That's it, two-legs, bring it here," she purred, her voice sweet as honey. "It's the only way to save your little manatee friend. We wouldn't want anything bad to happen to her, now, would we?"

Layla twisted her face into a look of nervous confusion. "If I give you the pearl, will you promise to let Silva go?"

"No!" Grace yelled out from behind her. She swam towards Layla, as if to stop her, but two huge alligators blocked her way, trapping her against the shore. Grace fought against their scaly tails, pushing and pulling to try and get past.

"You can't do it, Layla. Think what she'll do with the pearl's magic!" Grace shouted as the alligators snapped and snarled to keep her back.

"She'll release her siren sisters!" Emily cried out, sounding scared. "They'll hurt so many creatures."

Either Emily was a better actress than she thought, or she was really, truly frightened. Layla looked from her friends to Effluvia, who swished her tail impatiently.

Layla sighed with pretend disappointment. "It's the only way," she said, dropping the fake pearl into Effluvia's outstretched palm.

"Nooooooo!"
Grace
shrieked.
"Layla,
how could
you?" Emily
looked close to
tears.

Layla felt her own eyes welling up. She imagined how she would feel if she really had given Effluvia the pearl – how guilty and worried and scared – and she tried to show all of her feelings in her face. "You have to let Silva go," she said fiercely. "You promised."

Effluvia didn't even look at her, she

was too busy laughing as she clutched
her hands around the pearl. "Yes, yes."
She waved a hand lazily and the yellow
light disappeared from the alligators'
eyes. "You save your precious manatee
– none of that matters now. Finally, my
siren sisters will be FREE and we can rule
every inch of this ocean. With one spell,
everything I've dreamed of will finally
come true!" She opened her mouth to
sing, and Layla suddenly realised she
needed more time. If Effluvia used the
pearl's power now, she'd know she'd been
tricked – and she could capture Silva all
over again!

"What will you do first?" she croaked,

trying to sound terrified. Behind her back she waved her hand at Grace and Emily, gesturing for them to take Silva away.

Effluvia gave a happy sigh. "First I will take over Atlantis." She smiled dreamily. "Princess Marina and her family will all work for me!"

Layla glanced over her shoulder. Grace and Emily had one arm each around Silva and were speeding her to safety as quickly as they could.

"My sisters and I will make an army of sea creatures. No one will stop us!" Effluvia continued. Then she turned to Layla with a wicked gleam in her eye. "And you pesky Sea Keepers will be banished, for ever!"

She opened her mouth and sang:

"Golden Pearl, listen to me,

Set my siren sisters free!"

She cackled as she held the pearl high overhead. But nothing happened.

"What?" Effluvia snarled.

"Golden Pearl, listen to me,

Set my siren sisters free!" she chanted,

sounding desperate. Effluvia tried again and again, then flung the fake pearl down to the seabed in fury.

Layla had never seen the siren this angry. She quickly flicked her tail and swam after the others. They had to use the real pearl's power quickly, before Effluvia could find it.

"What have you done?" Effluvia screeched. Her furious shouts and screams echoed behind Layla as she swam. "You think you can trick ME? You'll pay for this!"

Layla kept her eyes fixed up ahead, where Valeria was hugging Silva. The others were already there. She just

needed to touch the Golden Pearl with them, then they could make the wish.

Effluvia opened her mouth and let out a high-pitched note that churned the river into a fierce whirlpool. The girls watched in horror as it travelled up to the surface where it was met by an answering roll of thunder. Effluvia had used her magic to start the storm!

Chapter Nine

As Effluvia raged and roared, so did the
storm. The water surged up and down.
Layla kept trying to swim towards
her friends, but it was like being on a
rollercoaster ride, the waves lifting her
high and then dropping her down so fast
it made her tummy flip. A huge wave
knocked into the friends, sending them
flying through the water.

"The pearl!" Grace gasped as it slipped from her grasp.

"Got it!" Layla cried as she dived forward to catch it. Now she just had to make it to her friends . . .

"You'll regret this!" Effluvia screamed above the thunder. "I'll get you, Sea Keepers!"

Grace, Layla and Emily ignored her and kept swimming towards each other. Finally, they all had their hands on the precious pearl.

"I wish the manatees could have a safe and easy migration!" Layla called.

The magical light disappeared from the pearl – and the storm disappeared with

it. "Nooooo!" shrieked Effluvia as the last wave surged towards her, sweeping her and the alligators down the river.

There was a moment's silence, then Silva piped up. "That was *sooooo* exciting!" she said. "Did you see when she made the storm come? I thought she was going to win for sure. But you were so brave. Are we going to get to migrate after all? How about the farewell party,

can you stay a little while?"

Everyone burst into giggles. Valeria wrapped her flippers around Silva and squeezed her tight. "Let's go find the rest of our herd," she said.

"The water should be calm and clear for the whole of your migration," Marina said. "The Golden Pearl will take care of that – no matter how slow you go!"

"And we can definitely have a party," Layla said. "I think we deserve one."

They all laughed and joked as they swam back to the herd.

"Did you see Effluvia's face . . ." Marina said, chuckling.

"She was so angry," Grace said.

"Your acting was really good!" Layla told her friends.

"I wasn't acting, I was really scared!" Emily admitted.

"I think you're the bravest people I know," Silva said. "You're my heroes!"

As they got back to the herd and told them what had happened, the manatees and mermaids burst into applause. Everyone clapped and cheered. The crabs clacked their pincers to make applause almost as loud as the storm's thunder.

"And from one adventure to the next!" Tia announced. "We normally gather to ask the sprits of the sea for a safe migration, but we already know you're going to have that, thanks to the Sea Keepers!"

"We'd better be on our way," said Valeria.

Marina opened her mouth and sang the farewell song that she'd tried to sing before. This time there were no interruptions!

The manatees set off and the mermaids and other creatures waved and wished them a good journey.

"Goodbye, Sea Keepers. I'll never forget you!" Silva said, tickling their cheeks with her whiskers as she gave them a kiss.

"Safe travels!" called Layla, waving.

"I wonder how long it will take them

to get there," said Emily, watching Silva swim off with her grandmother.

"For ever, if they swim at their usual pace," joked Grace.

Layla was still waving goodbye when Emily nudged her. "Something else will be starting soon!" she said.

"Nadia's play! I nearly forgot!" Layla grinned.

Then Marina said the magic words to send them home.

"Goodbye!" the girls called as the magic bubbled around them. In a blink, they were back at the seaside theatre, tucked out of sight behind the kiosk. The long line of people queuing for anoraks were all looking up in amazement as the black clouds disappeared and a beautiful rainbow stretched over the sky instead, curving behind the stone stage.

"Looks like the Golden Pearl worked on the storm here too!" Emily said in delight. "Nobody needs anoraks now."

"That saves the world from a bit more

plastic," Grace said happily.

"And means we won't get wet bums watching Nadia!" Layla added. They giggled as they went back to their seats.

"I can't wait for the show to begin," Emily said as they sat down.

Layla giggled as she grabbed her best friends' hands. "No matter how good the play is, today's best performances will be the ones we gave to defeat Effluvia!"

The End

Join Emily, Grace and Layla
for another adventure in ...

Seal Pup Party

Read on for a sneak peek!

Grace looked around the lounge
and grinned in glee. It was all so
Christmassy! The fir tree in the corner
was covered with baubles and twinkly
lights and there was holly draped over
the top of the fireplace. Grandad was
in his usual armchair, looking at his
phone, and her dog Barkley was laid out
in front of the cosy fire, snoring happily.
Just then, he sat up and pricked an ear.
A second later the doorbell rang and a

carol started from outside. "*Silent Night, Holy Night . . .*"

"Ooh, carol singers!" Grace's little brother Henry dropped his toy car and ran to the door.

"Those aren't carol singers," Grace said, barging ahead of him to open it.

Her best friends Emily and Layla were huddled on the doorstep. Behind them, the sea was dark and choppy, the waves splashing up on to the beach.

"*Sleep in heavenly peace!*" Layla sang loudly, flinging her arms out wide as Emily giggled.

"Get them in, quick, it's freezing out there!" Mum called from the kitchen.

Grace ushered her friends into the warm cottage and helped them hang up their coats and hats on the rack.

"Right, bakers, I've left everything out for you. Try not to make too much of a mess," Grace's mum said. It was Christmas Eve, and Emily and Layla had come round specially to make mince pies for Santa.

The kitchen was soon full of laughter and singing as the girls rolled out the pastry and filled it with delicious mincemeat. Grace had just put the mince pies in the oven when Henry gave a loud yelp from the lounge.

The girls rushed in to see what was

happening. Henry was standing by a pile of Christmas stockings, sucking his bleeding finger. "The holly spiked me!" he complained.

Layla went over to the fireplace to help. "Argh!" she cried out as she moved the holly.

Read
Seal Pup Party
to find out what adventures are in store for Emily, Grace and Layla!

Dive into a mermaid adventure!

The Mermaid's Dolphin
Coral Ripley

The Sea Unicorn
Coral Ripley

Coral Reef Rescue
Coral Ripley

Sea Turtle School
Coral Ripley

Penguin Island
Coral Ripley

Sea Otter
Summer Camp
Coral Ripley

The Rainbow Seahorse
Coral Ripley

Whale Song Wedding
Coral Ripley

The Missing Manatee
Coral Ripley

Coming Soon

Seal Pup Party
Coral Ripley

Starfish Sleepover
Coral Ripley

Love reading about animals?
Don't miss these great stories
by Tilda Kelly!